Dora's Chilly Day

NICKELODEON

DORA the EXPLORER

by Kiki Thorpe   illustrated by Steven Savitsky

SIMON AND SCHUSTER/NICKELODEON

Based on the TV series *Dora the Explorer* as seen on Nick Jr.

SIMON AND SCHUSTER

First published in Great Britain in 2005 by Simon & Schuster UK Ltd
1st Floor, 222 Gray's Inn Road, London WC1X 8HB

Originally published in the USA in 2004 by Simon Spotlight,
an imprint of Simon & Schuster Children's Division, New York.

A CIP catalogue record for this book is available from the British Library

ISBN 978-0-85707-430-0

Printed in China

10 9 8 7 6 5 4 3 2

Visit our websites: www.simonandschuster.co.uk
www.nick.co.uk

¡Hola! Today Boots and I are visiting *Abuela's* house.

Brrr! It's chilly today. *Abuela* is going to make a chilly day surprise! She needs milk, sugar, and chocolate . . .

Uh-oh! *Abuela* has run out of chocolate. She can't make the surprise without it!

Wait! I know where we can get some: the Chocolate Tree! Boots and I will go to the Chocolate Tree to get some chocolate for *Abuela.* Will you help us? Great!

First we'll need something to help us stay warm outside. Let's look in Backpack. Say "Backpack!"

Can you see something that will keep us warm? Right! Some mittens and hats will help us stay warm! Now we're ready to go and see our friend the Chocolate Tree.

Let's ask Map what the best way to the Chocolate Tree is.

Map says that to get to the Chocolate Tree we have to go over the Troll Bridge and through the Nutty Forest. *¡Vámonos!* Let's go!

Brrr! The wind is really strong. What a chilly day!
Look, there's Diego. I wonder what Diego likes to do on a chilly day . . .

Diego is bringing some straw to Mama Blue Bird so she can build a nice warm nest for her Blue Bird babies. Nice work, Diego! Come on! We're almost at the Troll Bridge.

We made it to the Troll Bridge. And there's the Grumpy Old Troll. What do you think the Grumpy Old Troll likes to do on a chilly day?

The Grumpy Old Troll likes to make up new riddles! And he has a special chilly day riddle for us:

"This riddle is tricky. You'll have to think twice.
When water freezes, it turns into . . ."

That's a hard one. Do you know the answer?

Ice, right! Yay! We solved the Troll's riddle. Now we can cross the Troll Bridge!

Look! There's our friend the Big Red Chicken. I wonder what the Big Red Chicken likes to do on a chilly day . . .

The Big Red Chicken is knitting a big red scarf! That will help him stay nice and warm.

Do you remember where we go next? That's right – the Nutty Forest! *Adiós,* Big Red Chicken!

Uh-oh. That's a very mucky mud puddle. We have to cross it to get to the Nutty Forest. Can you see a way to get to the other side?

We can use those stepping-stones.
Good thinking!

Mmmm! What's that delicious smell? It's coming from Tico's Tree House!

Tico likes to bake Nutty Butter
Cookies on a chilly day. And he has
some cookies for us! *Gracias,* Tico.
Come on, let's hurry. We're
almost there!

We made it! *Hola,* Chocolate Tree! *Abuela* needs three pieces of chocolate for her surprise. Can you see three pieces?

I can't wait to see what the chilly day surprise is. Let's hurry back to *Abuela's* house. Remember to keep an eye out for Swiper. That sneaky fox will try to swipe our chocolate. If you see him, say "Swiper, no swiping!"

Hooray! We brought the chocolate home to *Abuela*. Now she can make the chilly day surprise.

Abuela taught us a special chocolate song in Spanish.
While *Abuela* mixes in the chocolate, we can help her by
singing. Will you sing with us? Great!

¡Bate, bate - chocolate!
¡Bate, bate - chocolate!

Abuela's chilly day surprise is hot chocolate. *¡Delicioso!* I love drinking hot chocolate on a chilly day.

What do *you* like to do on a chilly day?